A SAM & FRIENDS MYSTERY

Lake Monster Mix-Up

MARY LABATT • **JO RIOUX**

KIDS CAN PRESS

Text © 2009 Mary Labatt
Illustrations © 2009 Jo Rioux

This is a work of fiction and any resemblance of characters to persons living or dead is purely coincidental.

Kids Can Press acknowledges the financial support of the Government of Ontario, through the Ontario Media Development Corporation's Ontario Book Initiative; the Ontario Arts Council; the Canada Council for the Arts; and the Government of Canada, through the BPIDP, for our publishing activity.

Published in Canada by
Kids Can Press Ltd.
29 Birch Avenue
Toronto, ON M4V 1E2

Published in the U.S. by
Kids Can Press Ltd.
2250 Military Road
Tonawanda, NY 14150

www.kidscanpress.com

Based on the book *The Secret of Sagawa Lake* by Mary Labatt.

Edited by Karen Li
Designed by Kathleen Gray
Printed and bound in China

The hardcover edition of this book is smyth sewn casebound.
The paperback edition of this book is limp sewn with a drawn-on cover.

CM 09 0 9 8 7 6 5 4 3 2 1
CM PA 09 0 9 8 7 6 5 4 3 2 1

Library and Archives Canada Cataloguing in Publication

Labatt, Mary, [date]
Lake monster mix-up / written by Mary Labatt ;
illustrated by Jo-Anne Rioux.

(A Sam & friends mystery)
Interest age level: For ages 7–10.
ISBN 978-1-55337-822-8 (bound). ISBN 978-1-55337-302-5 (pbk.)

I. Rioux, Jo-Anne II. Title. III. Series: Labatt, Mary, [date] . Sam & friends mystery.

PS8573.A135L35 2009   jC813'.54   C2008-907085-2

Kids Can Press is a *Corus*™ Entertainment company

Later that afternoon ...

I wish I could live with you.

What about my brother, Noel?

What a lout.

What's a lout?

A lummox. An oaf. A teenager.

You two look like you're having a conversation!

Hi, Mom.

Did your dad tell you the good news?

What news?

We're going to Sagawa Lake for the long weekend!

Sagawa Lake! It takes *hours* to get there!

Noel's complaining, too. I don't understand it.

There's nothing to do up there.

That's right! No cars. No telephone. Nothing but wilderness!

Bor-ing.

I hate the wilderness.

Don't bears live in the wilderness?

Come with me! Noel always brings a friend.

I'll ask if Beth can come, too!

Bears are worse than dog food.

I'll bring snacks ...

Maybe I can stand it for one weekend.

sigh

I'm sure the turn is coming up.

Look! There's the old ferry landing.

BUMP! Ba-BUMP!

VVRRRRRRRRRRRR

Ask about the secret.

What's the secret of the lake?

VVRRRRRRRRRRRRRRR

It's probably just an old campfire story.

Local people love to scare tourists like us.

VVRRRRRRRRRRRRRRRRRRRRRR

Don't start on the ghosts, Sam.

Sounds like a ghost.

Maybe it is a ghost.

Sam thinks some dead girl is calling to her lost love.

Oooo ... Oooo ... Oooo ...

It must be a sad story.

I love Beth. And I love ghosts!

Hear the loons?

Loons?

Oooo ... Oooo ...

Listen. Sounds sad, doesn't it?

Don't you dare get us into trouble, Sam.

I never got anybody into trouble in my life!

Late that night ...

They're driving me crazy. Why don't they shut up?

Sam wants the loons to shut up.

So do I.

What'll we do tomorrow?

I brought a book on northern trees ...

Jennie ...

What's so funny?

Now Sam wants *you* to shut up.

I bet she thinks that stuff is boring.

Worse than boring. Let's talk about mysteries.

Ouch.
There's something sticking out of this stupid wall.

Hmm ...
smells like damp old wood ... and leather?

sniff
sniff

Maybe it's a leather money pouch. Maybe it's the old trapper's gold hidden in the wall!

Got it!

click!

June 5, 1937.
My name is Ruth. The cabin is finally finished, and we've come to spend the summer on Sagawa Lake. This is my new diary.

Wow! Somebody's diary!

1937! That was ages ago!

Okay, someone wrote in this thing. Big deal. Skip the boring stuff.

She's ten years old! Like us!

It's like meeting someone from the past!

Did she say anything about a mystery?

We need time to read this, Sam. She wrote a lot.

Then I'm going to need a snack.

Into the early morning ...

Listen!

June 24, 1937.
I am frightened of the secret
of Sagawa Lake. My parents met an
old prospector who believed it.
He painted the face on the rock
to ward off the evil
in the lake.

Evil in the lake. That gives me a chill.

Yes! Gold is good, but a mystery is better!

The old guy asked if we were scared, didn't he?

Yeah.

Think about it. Being scared. Evil in the lake. Hmm ...

I know! It's a sea monster!

Or should I say a *lake monster.*

A lake monster!

The monster of Sagawa Lake!

Maybe Ruth says more about it!

Enough reading. I have to get a look at this thing. We'll need a boat.

Good morning! Pull up a chair.

I hope he made dill-pickle pancakes for breakfast!

You girls are up early. What are your plans today?

Can we take the rowboat? To explore the island?

As long as it's safe. I'll check it out after breakfast.

What a lovely way to enjoy the wilderness. But remember to wear life jackets.

And stay near shore.

Soon ...

Look. Maybe it's a river.

Get closer!

This is spooky.

The best things in life are spooky.

I see something ahead ...

It's only a painting!

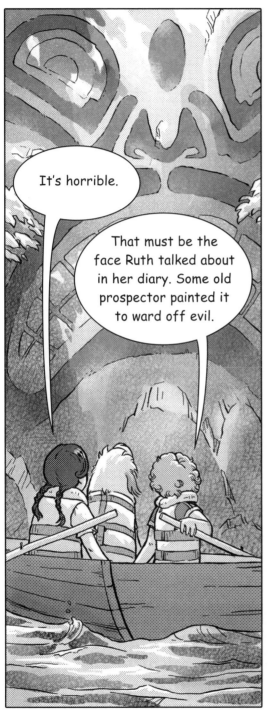

It's horrible.

That must be the face Ruth talked about in her diary. Some old prospector painted it to ward off evil.

That's it! I bet the monster lives farther up the river ...

... in that cave.

What kind of clues are you looking for?

A monster horn ... or claw ...

Maybe even one of his victims!

I'm going to be famous!

How can you be famous when you're eaten up?

Aha! I told you I'd find a clue.

Sam's found something!

Ruth was scared all summer. Look what she says here.

July 11, 1937.
Evil stalks Sagawa Lake at midnight. You must be indoors with the windows shut, lest it come in and grab you while you're sleeping.

Sleeping, huh?
Does this thing eat dogs?

It doesn't say anything
about dogs ...

Ruth says, "Evil walks on
Winnewago Island under
the full moon!"

But ...

There will be
a full moon
tonight!

That evening ...

A full moon.

Get ready, everybody. I'm going to tell a ghost story.

Long ago, two boys dared each other to sleep in a haunted castle. At the stroke of midnight, they heard a sound ...

I thought we were alone on this island.

RUSTLE RUSTLE

Maybe it's a bear. Mrs. Anderson said they had a bear once!

RUN!

Everybody inside!

It's a monster, Mom! There was a girl named Ruth! Her family built this cabin, and she says there's monster in the lake!

He walks on Winnewago Island at midnight!

Under the full moon!

Now that would make a good story! Maybe mine are getting a bit old.

Bedtime. The bear will be gone by morning.

Noel and Jason are never going to stop laughing at us.

We just need proof!

How are we going to get proof?

Let's go back to the cave!

This time, we're bringing the camera.

Early the next morning ...

Noel and Jason are still laughing at us. And Mom says to stay near the shore.

That's the plan. We'll paddle along the shore ...

... up the river and into the cave. This time, watch out for the bats!

Y-you're sure the monster won't be around?

Soon ...

Maybe he sleeps on the bottom —

Something's going on down there!

We've found an underwater city! Maybe those are underwater cars. We'll be famous!

W-we have to g-get out of here!

Wait! Where are they going?

I know what they are! They're dinosaur frogs.

Dinosaur frogs?

Yes! Like frogs left over from prehistoric times.

I don't want to be slurped up.

Relax.
The monsters are back in the cave, and we're ... Uh-oh!

Maybe I spoke too soon.

EEEEEEEEEEEEEEK!!!

SLAM!

It followed us!

There were two of them.

Maybe thousands.

Sam thinks the lake is full of those things!

That's the evil in the lake. Sagawa Lake is full of dinosaur frogs.

I can't believe these things aren't in my books.

I'm glad we're going home tomorrow. All we have to do is make it through the night.

Hey! Nobody took a picture! How can I be famous when I don't have anything to show the newspapers?

I'm not going back for photos, Sam. You can be famous for another case. Something safer.

Sam has a point. If we've only got one night, we should get some proof.

This is an important discovery, Jennie. Weird creatures left over from millions of years ago. It's fabulous!

Exactly!

What's so fabulous about it? I think being home would be really fabulous.

I'm taking that picture — tonight.

Do you think we should warn them? They could get slurped right off that dock.

Noel would laugh his head off.

The world won't miss a couple of teenagers anyway.

Later ...

Oooo ... Oooo ...

Oooo .... Oooo ...

SPLASH!

Those monsters will drag Beth back to the underwater city!

I'll save her!

WOOF WOOF!

SPLASH!
SPLASH!
SPLASH!

Run, Jennie!

Back at the cabin ...

That dog is crazy.

Absolutely nuts!!

No need to be insulting.

We are very sorry.

Just what were you two doing out of bed?

Tell her about the lake monsters, Jennie.

We found an old diary from 1937. It belonged to a girl named Ruth.

Well ... Ruth said she was scared of the evil in the lake.

And we thought we found out what the evil was.

Get to the cave part.

W-we found a cave along the river. And we saw something glowing under the water.

That was us! We were using underwater lights.

Ruth's diary said an old prospector was scared of something evil in the lake. He painted a huge face on a rock to ward off the evil spirits. We saw it!

That's fascinating! A diary from 1937. I'd like to see it.

Did you see the kids in the cave?

We don't pay any attention to rowboats. We just get on with our research.

What do you study?

We're studying the marine life here.

And I can promise you that there are no monsters in that lake!

That's what you think, Lady. Tell them what else we saw!

But there's more. When we left the cave, a huge shadow followed us all the way back to the dock!

That's Old Harry!

The next day ...

I hate to leave. I love it here.

Would she love the monsters?

There are no monsters, Sam!

I'm not so sure, Jennie. Ruth was scared of *something* in this lake.

Join Claire and her friends for action-packed fun!

Claire and the Bakery Thief

Claire, her dog, Bongo, and her best friend, Jet, must catch the Bakery Thief — a recipe for fun and adventure.
Written and illustrated by Janice Poon

Hardcover 978-1-55453-286-5
Paperback 978-1-55453-245-2

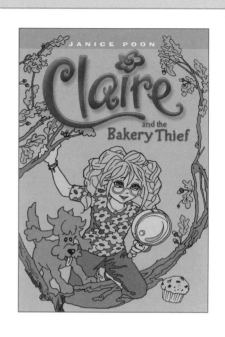

Claire and the Water Wish

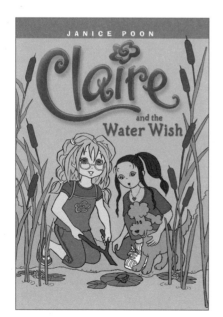

After Claire and Jet's friendship hits a bumpy spot, the girls need to put their differences aside to help bring the Lovesick Lake polluters to justice.
Written and illustrated by Janice Poon

Hardcover 978-1-55453-286-5
Paperback 978-1-55453-245-2